D0367244

Diary of an Adventurous Creeper

Book One: Creeper Chronicles

Mark Mulle

PUBLISHED BY:

Mark Mulle

Copyright © 2015

All rights reserved.

No part of this publication may be copied, reproduced in any format, by any means, electronic or otherwise, without prior consent from the copyright owner and publisher of this book.

Disclaimer

This is a work of fiction. Names, characters, businesses, places, events and incidents are either the products of the author's imagination or used in fictitious manner. Any resemblance to actual persons, living or dead, or actual events is purely coincidental.

Author's Note: This short story is for your reading pleasure. The characters in this "Minecraft Adventure Series" such as Steve, Endermen or Herobrine...etc are based on the Minecraft Game coming from Minecraft ®/TM & © 2009-2013 Mojang / Notch

Other books in the Diary of an Adventurous Creeper Series

Book Two: Journey to the End

Book Three: Dragon Savior

Table of Contents

DAY 1

Dear Diary,

My name is Carl the Creeper.

I am a very sad creeper because I'm all alone. There are no others like me. I don't have any friends.

Today, I stumbled upon the strangest thing. Cony the Cow was holding a small flashing box and looking at it making all sorts of poses. It was a very puzzling sight. I walked up to him and asked,

"Hey Cony, what are you doing?"

"Mooo...get away from me creeper...mooo." He said, and started to run.

"Hey, hold on. I just want to see what you're doing." I called after him, but he had run too far away from me.

Nobody liked me. I was called a green monster, lonely creep, wandering orphan and many more bad names. But what can I do? I'm just a sad green thing with no origins.

With a discouraged sigh, I started to walk back home wondering what that black box was, and why did Cony have to pose before each flashing.

DAY 2

Dear Diary,

I woke up to a very beautiful morning. The trees were evergreen and the water very clean. It was just the perfect day for me to enjoy the sun. I sat on my favorite chair in front of my house and looked around with the little of smile on my face.

Then, again, I saw Cony holding that same black box and this time he had Rowley the Rabbit, Sally the Slime, Silverfish Sidney, and Chima the Chicken with him.

They all surrounded him dancing and laughing. They were all posing together in front of the flashing little box and saying 'CHEESE!' What did 'CHEESE' even mean? I asked myself. Well, it didn't matter what it meant. Cony has a lot of friends now, and Cony didn't have many friends before.

Maybe if I get that black flashing box, then I might just have friends too. I thought hopefully.

Once inside my house, I headed straight for my library and began to read as many books as I could about flashing boxes.

DAY 3

Dear Diary,

A flashing box is actually called a camerax. I'd read from one of my books that it is a very rare item that takes pictures of anything, and can only be given by the Blaze Guardian in the heart of the Forgotten Nether Fortress when you wish for it. I should find this guardian, but instead of a camerax I would ask it to give me a family that would love me.

Today I began my quest to find the Blaze Guardian so I could get a family too. I needed two enchanted maps, one leading to The Lost Temple of Minelantis where I would find the second map that would lead to the Forgotten Nether Fortress. I decided to start looking in the mines.

I dug and dug, and dug deep down, but I couldn't find anything. Maybe I'm not looking in the right place, I thought to myself. I quickly left the mines to find Cony and ask him where he got the flashing box.

"Hey Cony, I promise I won't do anything to you. I just want to ask you a question." I said

"Mooo...what do you want?" Cony answered.

"Where did you get the flashing box?" I asked.

"My father gave it to me for my birthday. He wished for it in the Forgotten Nether Fortress. Good luck finding one...Mooo."

I didn't have any father to give me a camerax. I threw my pickaxe at a tree in anger and ran back home in tears.

DAY 4

Dear Diary,

Knock! Knock! There was a knock on my door. Who could that be? No one ever visits me, I thought.

I climbed down from my bed, slowly tip-toed to the door and looked through the peephole.

There was no one there. Are those lousy mobs playing a prank on me again? Well, there was only one way to find out.

I opened the door to find a small package at the doorstep. It had a note attached to it. I picked up the package and read the note. It said 'I hope you find what you're looking for, my friend.'

"My friend..." I said out loud. "I have a friend!" I shouted joyfully.

Placing the package on the table, I tore it open with great excitement and found the first map I needed. It was the map of the Lost Temple of Minelantis and had all the information I needed to get there. "Thank you, whoever you are." I muttered and began to prepare for my journey.

DAY 5

Dear Diary,

The map had a lot of information. It said the flashing box was called a camerax, and I would find it in the Forgotten Nether Fortress, but I needed to find the Nether map first which was in the underwater monument called The Lost

Temple of Minelantis. I've heard so many bad stories about the Nether world. There was lava instead of water, no trees, no sunshine, and there were deadly creatures.

To get to the Nether, I must first build a portal and find the Nether map. I went down into the mines to gather some coal for the torches I needed to light my way in the dark, as well as some iron and diamonds to craft armor and weapons. On my way, I met Rowley the Rabbit and Sally the Slime.

"Hello, guys." I greeted them with a smile.

"Cony told us you are looking for the Forgotten Nether Fortress." They said, grinning impishly.

"Yes, and I know where to find it." I replied.

"Really? Sally, did you hear that?" Rowley squealed.

"Can we come with you, please?" Sally begged.

"Sure, why not." I replied.

I was beginning to make friends, at last. Or so I thought.

DAY 6

Dear Diary,

Sally, Rowley, and I happily went into the jungle biome, the first leg of the journey to the Temple of Minelantis. We need to reach the Gibbous Temple where we intend to rest.

We reached the temple just before sunset. It was very big, round, and gloriously magnificent.

There were treasure chests with lots of good things inside and a board with a warning above the chests that read 'Do not be greedy. Take only one item stack each'. Rowley and I took a stack of golden apples each, but Sally took an entire iron armor set, a diamond sword and a stack of enchanted golden apple.

"No, Sally!" Rowley shouted as the entire temple began to shake.

We got attacked by zombies, spiders, and skeletons. Barely managing to fight our way through those horrible creatures, we finally made it out of the temple.

I turned to Sally, and said angrily, "If you'll be a trouble, then I think we should part ways now."

We made camp in the Savannah biome. Sally was looking very angry, but I decided to ignore her. We ate some fish, and went to sleep.

DAY 7

Dear Diary,

The sound of my belly rumbling woke me up from a dreamless sleep. I looked around, but there was no one in sight, my supplies bag was gone, and so were Rowley and

Sally. They did leave a note saying, 'Sorry Buddy, but you were the one that said we should part ways if we'd cause you more trouble. P.S. Good luck finding the Forgotten Nether Fortress. Ha-ha-ha!'

They had taken my weapon, my food...and...Oh! My map too! I sat under a tree and cried. I did not know how to find my way back home. I was so lost, and all alone. Something fell from above and hit me hard on the head before landing in front of me. Lo and behold! It was an apple. I squealed joyfully and ate it all up.

I made an axe from wood, and throughout the day, I picked apples and caught fish. Soon, I gathered supplies, made a stone sword and continued my journey. I could remember some key clues from the map, but did not know in which direction to head, so I decided to follow the clouds which were going west, or so I believed.

DAY 8

Dear Diary,

It was a very rainy day, and I feel very tired. I walked over three thousand blocks into the Dusty Deserts before I found some water and some sugar cane. I made some discoveries too. First, I could breathe underwater. I didn't know how it happened, and I didn't have this ability before, but I can breathe underwater now. Things were starting to work out in my favor.

With my new found ability, I went fishing where I made the most interesting discovery. I found The Lost Temple of Minelantis. It was the largest temple I had ever seen, made with the most beautiful prismarine blocks. I made it! My heart almost exploded with joy.

It was protected by fifteen guardians shooting laser beams at whoever got close. It's best to avoid them for now, I thought. I swam away from the temple to the land. In the distance, I could see some skeletons jockeys heading in my direction and I quickly look for a shelter away from the mobs. I did not want to lose more energy fighting them, and they could easily finish me given it was just me against a lot of them.

DAY 9

Dear Diary,

My journey so far has been difficult, but I will not give up. I will find the Blaze Guardian so I could wish for a family, and also prove to everyone that I am strong and do not need their friendship anymore.

I went back into the ocean to check on those guardians and see how I could get past them. I was shocked to see Rowley and Sally there too, but none of them saw me. They were giving the guardians something. I carefully moved closer and saw what it was, an emerald. So that was the token the guardians needed to grant passage.

Luckily, I had some emeralds too that I'd mined earlier.

"What brings you here, traveler?" One of the guardians asked.

"I seek to see the elders." I replied confidently.

"Give me your token." The guardian held out his hand and I placed the emerald.

I was allowed into the temple immediately.

DAY 10

Dear Diary,

I was beyond exhausted by the time I got past the temple gates. I had to rest for a while to regain all my energy and regenerate health.

I found the three elders of the temple in the main chambers. They looked like giant white fish with spikes coming out of their bodies.

"What do you seek, traveler?" one of the elders asked.

"I...I am looking for the Nether map." I replied, feeling very nervous.

"What makes you think you can get it?" They asked.

"The truth is that I'm looking for the Nether map so I can wish for a family from the Blaze Guardian." I admitted.

"Very well, then. Let the test begin." The elders said, and shot me with a loud and bright beam of light from their eyes.

DAY 11

Dear Diary,

It was pitch black and gravely silent around me. I didn't know where I was, and neither could I remember how I got there. There was a trickling sound of water that seemed to be coming from behind me. It took a little while before I was able to see a little bit in the dark. I got to my feet and walked towards the sound.

I found a button on a wall and pressed. The entire place lit up. I was in some sort of a maze.

I recalled the guardians saying 'let the test begin' before I found myself there. Again, I had nothing with me, no tools, no weapons, and no food.

I began to navigate the maze looking for anything I could find. My wandering brought me to a large room made of quartz. There were chests lining the walls, diamond blocks, gold blocks, emeralds, and armor among the many treasures around the room.

There was a sign on the wall with a riddle on it – 'On two legs he walks, the mighty looter, slayer of dragons and bane of us all.' Who walks on two legs, steals from mobs, and kills dragons? I asked myself. There could only be one answer.

"Herobrine!" I shouted and a mysterious door opened in front of me.

The three elders were waiting for me as I stepped in through the door.

"The Nether map is now yours. Use it wisely," said the elders.

I got the Nether map, my tools and supplies returned, and I was on my way to the Nether world.

DAY 12

Dear Diary,

The Nether map was especially difficult to find because it held all the secrets and treasures of the Nether world. It was a very sacred map, and I was glad it was in my possession.

To get to the Nether world, I must first create a portal and to create the portal, I must find the obsidian block.

I was down in the mines digging up obsidian when an odd thought came to my mind. Could there be others like me out there? Surely I cannot be the only one of my kind.

I never had any parents like the other mobs. I just woke up one day, and found myself in the middle of the wild-flower biome. I walked around for days, eventually finding the right spot and building a house close to the sea at the edge of the forest and began to live my life.

Bingo! I found the obsidian blocks and built the portal. All that was left was light it and pass through. I felt very nervous and scared. Will I make it out alive? Will I find what I'm looking for?

With grim determination, I lit the portal and stepped inside.

DAY 13

Dear Diary,

I was finally in the Nether world. Lucky enough, the portal brought me into an underground cave. I ate some fish, sharpened my tools, and rested before going out into the terrors of the Nether to complete my quest.

The Nether was my worst nightmares come true. There were many creatures that I'd never seen before. There were no trees, no open sky, and no water among other things. There were pools or lava everywhere with small magma cubes hopping around them, gangs of zombie pigmen wreaking havoc on anything they find. I should avoid them at all cost.

I walked up to the magma cube since they looked less hostile.

"Uhh...hello." I called out.

Blop! Blop! Blop! One large cube hopped forward from the crowd.

"What are you?" It asked.

"My name is Carl. I am from the Overworld." I replied.

"We don't see many mobs from the Overworld in the Nether. What brings you here?"

"I am searching for the neth –"

I was about to reveal what I was searching for when I noticed the other cubes hopping closer. Before I could grasp what was going on, they were trying to push me into a lava pool. I quickly grabbed my sword, hit them a couple of times and began to run.

DAY 14

Dear Diary,

I had no choice but to return to my cave base in the Nether. That was the only safe place I could be. I would die if I went out there again.

There was no knowing whether it was day or night in the Nether, but given the time I had spent down in my base, it was long enough to be a whole day or night. I came up with a counting method to determine the time.

I was starting to go crazy. My food was running out, and I was too afraid to go out.

Boom, boom, boom! Bam, bam! A loud noise came from my cave entrance. I quickly retreated to the depths of the cave in fear.

In came Rowley the Rabbit, this time he was with Chima the Chicken, and Danny the Dog. I grabbed my sword and approached them confidently. I was prepared to defend myself should they try to harm me.

"What do you want?" I asked angrily.

"Oh...w-w-we...we didn't know you were in here." Danny stammered. He had never been able to talk smoothly like everyone else without stammering.

I pointed my sword at them in an attempt to scare them. After all, I was stronger than they were.

"Get out of here. This is my territory." I hissed.

"We just want protection! It's too...dangerous out there." Chima clucked.

"Please let us stay. We promise to share our goodies with you." Rowley said.

"Have Rowley told you all what he and Sally did to me? "I asked angrily.

I wanted to kick them out of the cave, but then I thought about all the horrible things that could happen to them out there. They may be mean, sly and clever, but they were no match for the horrors of the Nether.

With a sigh, I put down my sword and allowed them to stay. "You may stay in that corner...and don't come near me." I warned.

"Jolly good Carl! Thank you!" They all cheered.

DAY 15

Dear Diary,

I woke up from sleep and found my not-so-welcome companions sitting in their assigned corner. I quickly checked my supplies and found everything intact. Whew! They didn't play me again.

"We're sorry we abandoned you the other day, Carl." Rowley said. "Sally made me do it. She got greedy back in the Gibbous Temple. Sally said we must leave you."

"You may have left me, but I'm here now, and giving you shelter." I replied smugly. "Where's Sally now?" I asked.

"She didn't make it. We tried to steal the Nether map from the elder guardians in Minelantis. I managed to escape, but Sally couldn't and was taken prisoner by the guardians. I don't want to be bad anymore." He said quietly.

"I see you've learnt your lesson. You may join me in my quest if you wish but on one condition. You will play by my rules."

"Y-yes, Carl. We all need to find some treasure, and so w-we must work together." Danny stammered.

"Alright then, we go out tomorrow. For now, let's study the map more and plan our strategies." I instructed.

We crafted stronger armor and weapons with the materials we had and enchanted them.

DAY 16

Dear Diary,

We left our base as soon as we detected it was morning and began to search for The Forgotten Nether Fortress. I felt more confident and courageous than I did before my alliance with Rowley, Chima, and Danny.

Rowley is not a bad rabbit; he just hung around bad company. Chima is a witty little chicken that loved to swim and play parkour in the Cloud Village. She also liked to groom her fluffy white feathers. Danny is a snooty dog that thinks he's smarter than everyone, though he seems a bit humbled now.

We fought a lot of magma cubes and collected some magma cream which we ate for fire resistance as we'd read in the survival notes attached to the Nether map. As long as we ate magma cream, fire won't hurt us.

Surprisingly enough, we didn't have any encounters with the zombie pigmen on the path we took. We walked seven thousand blocks before we dug an underground shelter to rest for the night.

DAY 17

Dear Diary,

Danny the Dog hurt one of his legs today. He got hit by a Ghast fireball. He couldn't walk so we had to carry him around in a bag. We were attacked by one very huge Ghast that kept firing at us nonstop. It was flying around rapidly so we could not shoot it down.

We had to hide behind netherrack structures to avoid getting hit directly, but poor Danny could not escape the awful fireball.

We found a cave near a large lava pool. It was not very big, but safe enough to protect us from the Ghast's fury.

"Quick, get Danny inside." I said to Rowley and Chima.

"What about you?" Rowley asked.

"I will be fine. I cannot let the Ghast get here." I replied.

As they went inside the cave, I rushed to lead away the Ghast that followed us. There were many small lava pools around, and a small misstep would have me falling into the hot lava. An idea suddenly popped into my head.

As the Ghast was shooting the fireballs, I tried to deflect them with my sword. First try, second try, and on the third try, I successfully redirected the fireball back at the Ghast instantly vanquishing it.

Triumphant at last, I went back to the cave where Danny had already been healed with an enchanted golden apple and they were all happy to see that I was alive.

DAY 18

Dear Diary,

After that scary mob battle with the Ghast yesterday, none of us wanted to go out. Danny was still shaking with fear, his fur stood straight like little needles. I felt like giving up, but I really needed to find others like me.

"Do you still want to continue this quest, Carl?" Asked Chima.

"Yes. I need to find others like me. I'm sick of being alone." I replied.

"We all have parents, brothers, and sisters except you. And you are a good mob. I will stand by you until you find what you are looking for." Chima said.

"You're a hero, Carl. I will stand by you." Said Rowley.

"M-me too, y-you just saved m-my life." Said Danny.

I began to cry because I was so happy. No one has ever supported me like that. I was really making friends. They gathered around me and gave me a big hug.

That day, we danced by the fire, ate fish and apples, and celebrated our newfound friendship.

DAY 19

Dear Dairy,

In the morning, we left our cave. We were out of enchanted apples, so we'd have to rely on magma cream for protection. We hunted more magma cubes and stocked up our magma cream supply.

We didn't walk for very long when the Nether map in my hand began to glow a little. As we walked forward, the glow intensity started to increase. We walked faster as the map glowed even more and we came to a huge magnificent structure. The Forgotten Nether Fortress stood before us.

"Cluck, cluck, cluck! We made it!" Chima exclaimed happily.

We all jumped and rejoiced momentarily before focusing our attention on the Wither Skeleton guards around the fortress. We had read about them in the map notes. They were very cruel mobs that struck down whoever got close to the fortress, but like all other guards, giving them a token – a Ghast tear, in this case – will have them grant passage.

"I-i-its m-magnificent!" said Danny in astonishment.

I approached them holding the Ghast tear up so they could see it and gave it to one of the Wither Skeleton guards. The doors instantly opened and we entered.

DAY 20

Dear Diary,

Inside the Nether Fortress was nothing like what I'd read. It was much darker and dangerous in real-life. There were many chambers with locked iron doors, but the chamber we were to look for was the Lapis Chamber. A chamber said to be full of lapis lazuli and gold blocks. Inside of that chamber lives the Blaze Guardian.

We walked past the Quartz Chamber, the Mushroom Chamber and the Wart Chamber until we came to the Cake Chamber and went inside. The chamber was not just filled with cakes; it had pumpkin pies, cookies, baked potatoes, and delicious cooked salmon and golden carrots.

We were all very hungry, but instead of eating right away, we looked around for warnings, in case the food was a trap. When we didn't find any warnings, I headed straight for the baked potatoes. Rowley went for the golden carrots, Chima had as many cookies as she could have, and Danny ate cooked salmon until he could no longer move. We fell asleep afterward.

DAY 21

Dear Diary,

Eating the most delicious food coupled with the most peaceful sleep, my friends and I were ever ready to find the Lapis Chamber and complete our quest. The fortress was very quiet, yet trap-laden. Chima helped us disable all the pressure plates around and we moved safely.

We found the Lapis Chamber at last, but it was closed. We looked around, read the map notes again and again hoping to find clues on how to open the door, but found nothing.

"A-a-and we're so c-close." Said Danny.

I looked at the map again. I saw and arrow pointing down at a spot in front of the door. I quickly used my pickaxe and dug out a single block. I flipped the switch I found in the hole and BINGO! The doors opened and we went into the Lapis Chamber.

The Lapis Chamber was not like the other chambers. It was about five times bigger and brighter. There were wooden chests and ender chests – magical chests that keep the most priceless of treasures.

The Lapis Chamber got filled up with some kind of a toxic gas.

I started to feel dizzy, and my feet could no longer hold me. I fell to the ground and just before my eyes closed, I saw my friends fall too. There came total darkness.

DAY 22

Dear Diary,

"W-w-what h-happened?" Danny's voice came through the darkness.

I slowly opened my eyes. I was still in the Lapis Chamber and very confused. Chima and Danny were there too, but Rowley was missing.

"Where's Rowley?" I asked.

"We don't know. We woke up and he was gone." Chima replied.

Could he have been taken by something or someone? Was he killed? Did he leave us here? All sorts of thoughts crossed my mind of how Rowley went missing.

"D-did he abandon us?" Danny asked

"No, Rowley is a changed person. He would not abandon us." I assured him.

"Look! There's Rowley's bag, and his bow and arrow." Cried Chima. "Oh, poor Rowley. What happened to him?"

Rowley's bag was lying on the chamber floor with all its contents scattered about. That convinced me that Rowley had been taken.

"We have to find him. I hope he's alright." I said.

"Oh, Rowley!" Chima cried again.

We left the Lapis Chamber and began to search for our friend.

DAY 23

Dear Diary,

We ran through the halls calling out Rowley's name. We searched as many chambers as we could find, but he was nowhere to be found.

"O-over here!" Danny called out.

We rushed to where he was standing but by the time we got there he was nowhere in sight. There was a paper on the floor in a corner. I picked up the paper and read, 'Help Me!' The paper was wrinkly, and the ink smudged all over.

"This has got to be from Rowley." Said Chima.

"Who c-could have t-t-taken him?" Danny asked.

"I did!" a voice said.

'On two legs he walks, the mighty looter, slayer of dragons, and bane of us all' As I remembered those words, I realized it was Herobrine. The fearsome mob hunter.

"I took your friend, and I'm going to make rabbit stew with him, the best meal in the world." Said Herobrine.

"We will never let you hurt Rowley!" Chima shouted.

"Shut up, you noisy chicken!" Herobrine shouted back. "I will make chicken soup with you too, and I will make the dog my slave. And you creeper, I can't cook you, but I will hand you over to my ocelots. Ha-ha-ha-ha!" Herobrine all of a sudden appeared and started charging towards us.

"Run!" I shouted.

We ran as fast as we could and he chased us. Suddenly, the running steps behind me stopped. I looked back and there was no one there. Herobrine had taken Danny and Chima.

"Nooooo!" I shouted.

DAY 24

Dear Diary,

All my friends were gone. I had searched everywhere within the fortress for them, but I couldn't find them.

I have to do whatever it takes to save them, and the Blaze Guardian might know something that would help. I just have to find him before it's too late.

According to the Nether Map, the guardian is in the heart of the fortress, meaning he is in the Lapis Chamber. But, why didn't we see him in the Lapis Chamber? I thought.

I checked my map notes for more information on the Blaze Guardian. It said; the Blaze Guardian only reveals himself when the ender chest containing the treasures is touched. He will test the seeker. If the seeker has a pure heart, the guardian will give him what he seeks. If the seeker is found unworthy, however, the seeker is teleported out of the fortress by the guardian.

I gathered up my bag and ran straight to the Lapis Chamber.

DAY 25

Dear Diary,

The Lapis Chamber was empty as expected when I got there. I slowly approached the ender chest, but before I even touched it, a bright light flashed, and the Blaze Guardian appeared.

The Blaze Guardian was very beautiful, bright yellow and fiery.

"What do you seek, traveler?" The guardian asked.

"I want to save my friends." I replied.

"That is not what you seek." He said. "What do you seek, traveler?" He asked again.

"I want to wish for a family." I answered.

"You can only choose one. Choose to save your friends, or choose to have a family. Choose carefully, traveler." Said the Blaze Guardian.

It was a tough choice to make. Rowley, Chima, and Danny have fought by my side. Without them, I would never have made it to the Forgotten Fortress. It didn't matter as much if there were others like me. I was not alone anymore, and my friends needed to be saved.

"I choose to save my friends." I answered.

"So shall it be." Said the guardian as he disappeared.

DAY 26

Dear Diary,

The last thing I remember was the guardian disappearing after I had chosen my wish. I woke up outside the Lapis

Chamber. I felt very sad and disappointed. My wish had not been granted. I thought.

I felt something move in my chest, followed by a slow ticking sound. Tick, tick, tick, tock, tick, tock! I was very confused.

"Your wish has been granted. You now have the power to save your friends. Good luck, traveler." A voice said. It was the Blaze Guardian's voice.

"I don't understand." I called out. "I thought you would help me save them."

I should have been more specific in my wish. What power did I have that could enable me save them? Could it be the thing ticking inside my chest?

I was able to move faster than before, and I had gained stealth as well. My footsteps were very silent.

DAY 27

Dear Diary,

I left the Forgotten Fortress to find my friends. I checked the Nether Map for clues, and there was a spot marked with 'H'. That could be Herobrine's lair, I thought.

There were many Ghasts flying above me, but they didn't attack. The Magma Cubes and Zombie Pigmen didn't even acknowledge my presence. I really did get a new power, I thought. It made me feel stronger, and more confident.

I reached a tall nether brick structure surrounded with Glowstones. This has to be Herobrine's lair.

I entered and the thing in my chest started to tick faster. The further I went in, the faster, and louder it ticked. I went up a long spiral staircase and reached an open room.

"Carl!" Chima exclaimed.

They were alive but behind iron bars. I ran towards them to break the bars, but Rowley shouted a warning. "Look behind you!" he said.

I quickly turned around, and Herobrine was standing there.

"Well, well, well, look who's joined the party." Said Herobrine.

As Herobrine walked closer to me, my body began to shake violently, and the ticking sound got louder and louder and louder.

BOOM, BOOM, BOOM!

DAY 28

Dear Diary,

Am I dead? Was I dreaming? I woke up in the Lapis Chamber. The ticking had stopped, but I was a little confused. Rowley, Chima, and Danny ran up to me and hugged me tightly.

"I am so happy; you're alright." Said Rowley

"You got hurt pretty bad, but the Blaze Guardian teleported us here in time to heal you." Said Chima.

"What happened in Herobrine's lair?" I asked.

"You blew him up. You defeated Herobrine and saved us. You're a true hero, Carl." Said Rowley.

"T-t-the Blaze Guardian s-said you chose to save us instead of having a f-family." Said Danny.

"Will you still be my friends even though I still don't have a family?" I asked.

They laughed and said in unison, "You are part of our family now, Carl."

They hugged me again, and we left the Forgotten Fortress to find our way home.

DAY 29

Dear Diary,

There were many mobs there to greet us when we stepped out of the portal and into the Overworld. Cony the

Cow, Catherine the Cat, Paul the Pig, Silverfish Sidney, and many others were cheering.

A tall dark mob with purple magical dust flying around him stepped forth from the crowd and smiled at me.

"Hello Carl, I'm Edward the Enderman. I have watched over you for a very long time." He said warmly.

"Really? You gave me the map of the Lost Temple of Minelantis" I shouted joyfully.

"Yes, and I am proud to see that you have returned safely, and have got what you were looking for." He said.

"Oh thank you, Edward." I said.

"C-carl, l-look!" Danny squealed.

I turned around, and to my bewilderment, there were two creepers that looked exactly like me walking toward us.

"Hello, Carl, we're your family. I am Camilla, your mother." Said one of them.

"And I am Marcellus, your father." Said the other creeper.

"How is this possible? I was only granted one wish." I said.

"The Blaze Guardian initially granted you a single wish, but your courage, honesty and selflessness made him grant you another. We lost you when you were still a baby." My mother said.

"We have been looking for you ever since. The Blaze Guardian came to us one day and told us where to find you." My father added.

I was so happy I started to cry, and they all embraced me lovingly.

DAY 30

Dear Diary,

Exactly a month ago, I was the saddest mob in the world, but look at me now. I'm the happiest creeper you'd ever meet. I have a beautiful and devoted mother, a strong and loving father, and my best friends, Rowley, Chima, and Danny…oh, there's Sally too.

She was released by the Elder Guardians after she promised to be a better mob. She apologized for all the things she'd done and now she is our best friend too.

All the mobs in the Overworld liked me even more when they heard about my great adventures. I was an Overworld hero and the coolest guy in my school. Yes, they let me go to school now.

My mother gave me a Camerax. I took so many pictures which I framed and hung all around my room.

With great courage and patience come great things. Never give up.

I have to go now. I don't want to be late for my picnic with Danny, Rowley, Sally and Chima. Goodbye then.

Sincerely,
Carl the Creeper

Other books in the Diary of an Adventurous Creeper Series